The publishers are grateful for permission to reproduce the following material:

Reprinted with the permission of Four Winds Press, an imprint of Macmillan Publishing Company from *The Shepherd Boy* by Kim Lewis. Copyright © 1990 Kim Lewis.

From *The Best of Aesop's Fables* retold by Margaret Clark; illustrated by Charlotte Voake. Text copyright © 1990 by Margaret Clark; illustrations copyright © 1990 by Charlotte Voake. By permission of Little, Brown and Company.

From *Where's Waldo: The Magnificent Poster Book* by Martin Handford. Copyright © 1991 by Martin Handford. By permission of Little, Brown and Company.

Excerpts and illustrations from *Michael Foreman's Mother Goose,* text copyright © 1991 by Walker Books Limited, illustrations copyright © 1991 by Michael Foreman, reprinted by permission of Harcourt Brace & Company.

Reprinted with the permission of Macmillan Publishing Company from *Little Pig's Tale* by Nigel Gray, illustrated by Mary Rees. Text copyright © 1990 Nigel Gray. Illustrations copyright © 1990 Mary Rees.

From the book *Alice's Adventures in Wonderland* by Lewis Carroll. Illustrations copyright © 1988 by Anthony Browne. Published in the United States by Alfred A. Knopf, Inc., a division of Random House, Inc. Used by permission of the publisher. All rights reserved.

Silly Goose. Copyright © 1986 by Jan Ormerod. By permission of Lothrop, Lee & Shepard Books, a division of William Morrow & Company, Inc.

Text copyright © year of publication of individual authors.
Illustrations copyright © year of publication of individual illustrators.
Cover illustration copyright © 1994 by Helen Oxenbury.
Title page illustration copyright © 1985 by Helen Oxenbury.

All rights reserved.

First U.S. edition 1995

Library of Congress Cataloging-in-Publication Data is available.
Library of Congress Catalog Card Number 91-71859

ISBN 1-56402-495-4

2 4 6 8 10 9 7 5 3 1

Printed in Hong Kong

Candlewick Press
2067 Massachusetts Avenue
Cambridge, Massachusetts 02140

BIG
BEAR'S
TREASURY

VOLUME FOUR

*A Children's
Anthology*

CANDLEWICK PRESS
CAMBRIDGE, MASSACHUSETTS

CONTENTS

Once again Big Bear has been having a wonderful time—choosing over thirty best-loved books and putting them into one big book, a book of books. This is the fourth of Big Bear's collections and, like all the others, it's brimful of treasure. With every turn of the page you can discover more gems by the world's finest authors and illustrators for children.

Many of the stories, extracts, and poems in this book also exist in books of their own. Some you might have at home, or know from school. Others, you may want to find in nearby bookstores or libraries. If you find selections you especially like, you can also go on a treasure hunt for other books by the same writers and artists.

Exploring this book is like a real adventure. You don't have to read it in the ordinary way. You can start it in the middle and finish it at the beginning if you like. It makes no difference—every page holds new surprises, new magic. Big Bear welcomes you to another children's treasury, and hopes you too will have a wonderful time.

Monday Run-Day

by Nick Sharratt

Monday run-day

Tuesday snooze-day

Friday tie-day

Saturday splatter-day

Wednesday friends-day   Thursday **grrrs**-day

Sunday bun-day

9

The Shepherd Boy
by Kim Lewis

James's father was a shepherd. Every day he got up very early, took his crook and his collie, and went off to see his sheep. James longed to be a shepherd too.

"You'll have to wait until you're a little older," his father said.

So every day James watched and waited.

James watched and waited all through spring. He watched as the new lambs were born and saw them grow big and strong.

James watched and waited all through summer. He watched his father clip the sheep and saw his mother pack the sacks of wool.

James watched and waited all through autumn. He watched his mother help to wean the lambs and saw his father dip the sheep.

On market day, James waited while the lambs were sold and heard the farmers talk of winter.

When snow fell, James watched his father feed the hungry sheep near the house and saw him take hay on the tractor to the sheep on the hill. Then James waited for his father to come home for dinner.

On Christmas Day, James and his father and mother opened their presents under the tree. James found a crook and a cap and a brand-new dog whistle of his very own.

In a basket in the barn, James found a collie puppy. James's father read the card on the puppy's neck.

It said: *My name is Jess. I belong to a shepherd boy called James.*

Then James and his
father went off to the
fields together.

When spring
came again,
James got up
very early.
He took his crook and
his cap, and called Jess
with his whistle.

my name is Jess.
I belong to a
shepherd Boy
called James.
XX

by William Mayne
HOB AND THE

Hob lies in his cozy place underneath the stairs.

He hears Mr. say to a visitor, "This is Mrs., here are Boy and Girl and Baby. And in there is Hob, who is imaginary."

Hob puts out his head. "I'm not," he says. No one hears him. "I wish Hob was more real," he says.

"Told you so." Birdie laughs. "Hob isn't really there."

Hob scowls, feeling angry. He goes to sleep again. He wakes up feeling sad. Something is not right. He hears Boy and Girl quarreling at dinner about the last raisin bun, and Baby cries, and someone gets a slap.

"Hob can tell," says Hob, "bad times have come. Today they will give me the last present." They give him something every night. He thinks it will be things to wear, and if it is he will have to leave.

"It happens to Hob," he says. He stomps around the room. He slams the door of his closet.

He trips over something in the corner of the room. "Watch your step, Hob," growls Birdie.

"What has tripped Hob?" says Hob. "If that's the best they can do for me I'll be glad to go."

"Temper, temper," says Birdie. And Hob understands his bad feelings.

"I'm not mad," he says. "Hob is never angry. Hob is calm. But someone's temper has been lost and left lying on the floor."

"You leave me alone," says Temper, in a horrible way. "Or you'll be sorry, sorry, sorry."

Hob steps back. It is a bad temper he has found. He must be careful.

"Steady, Hob," he says. "Hob, think."

Hob thinks. He knows he must get rid of Temper. But the way to do it is very hard for him.

"Birdie," he says, "Hob can't do it all alone."

"I can't do it at all," says Birdie. "Get rid of it. If it comes near me my feathers will fall out."

"We have to count backward," says Hob. "From five-and-twenty, like blackbirds in a pie. I can't count all alone. You start, feather duster, with the biggest number."

TEMPER

illustrated by
Patrick Benson

Hob and Birdie go on counting. They must not get it wrong. "Eighteen, seventeen," they say.

Temper stands on the porch. "Eight, seven," say Hob and Birdie.

Temper gets to the garden gate. "Three, two, one," say Hob and Birdie. "Zero."

"Liftoff," says Temper, and goes stomping down the road.

"Thank you, Birdie," says Hob. He takes his reward, the buttery raisin bun Boy and Girl fought over. He gives Birdie raisins from it.

"One," says Birdie.

"Which is it?" says Birdie. "Twenty-five," says Hob, "I think."

Birdie says, "Twenty-five." Hob thinks it over and says, "Twenty-four." He wakes Birdie, and she says, "Twenty-three." Temper begins to move toward the door.

"Two," says Hob.

"Three," says the clock.

THE WIZARD'S CAT

"Hello, cat."

"I wish I weren't a cat.
I'm tired of that."

**"Who would you
like to be?"**

"Like to be? Someone
better than me!"

**"Al-a-kazam! Al-a-kazee!
Be a sailor on the sea!"**

"No! No! The sea's
too rough for me!"

**"Fiddle-de-dee!
Now you shall be
a monkey up a tree!"**

"No! No!
The tree's too
high for me!"

**"Grumble, rumble,
fo-fum-fee!
What about a bumble bee?"**

by Colin and Jacqui Hawkins

**"Hippity hoppity
skippity roo!
Be a rabbit—that's
best for you!"**

"No!
I don't think
it's funny
being a bunny!"

**"Then split! splat!
Be a wizard's cat!"**

"Yes, I like that!"

"Happy now?"

"Yes, now I can see
it's best to be me!"

"No! No!
I don't want hairy knees,
and flowers make me sneeze!"

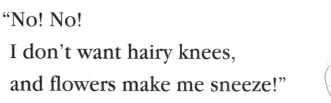

17

singing

Giving
by Shirley Hughes

waving

I gave Mom a present on her birthday, all wrapped up in pretty paper. And she gave me a big kiss.

I gave Dad a very special picture that I painted at play group. And he gave me a ride on his shoulders most of the way home.

sleeping

telling

listening

thinking

kicking

| eating | skipping | dancing | washing | smelling |

I gave the baby some
slices of my apple.
We ate them sitting
under the table.
At dinnertime the
baby gave me two of
his soggy bread crusts.
That wasn't much of a present!
You can give someone an angry look or
a big smile! You can give a tea party . . .
or a seat on a crowded bus.

| yawning | stroking | giving | writing | tearing |

singing

shouting

giving

crying

waving

On my birthday Grandma and Grandpa gave me
a beautiful doll's carriage. I said "Thank you,"
and gave them each a big hug.
And I gave my dear Bemily a ride
in it, all the way down the garden
path and back again.
I tried to give
the cat a ride
too, but she
gave me a
nasty scratch!

sleeping

telling

listening

thinking

kicking

eating

skipping

dancing

washing

smelling

So Dad had to give my poor arm a kiss and a Band-Aid. Sometimes, just when I've built a big castle out of blocks, the baby comes along and gives it a big swipe! And it all falls down. Then I feel like giving the baby a big swipe too. But I don't, because he *is* my baby brother, after all.

yawning

stroking

giving

writing

tearing

THE MOST OBEDIENT DOG

The most obedient dog in the world was waiting for something to happen when Harry came up the path.
"Hello, boy," said Harry.
The most obedient dog in the world wagged his tail and started to follow Harry.
"No . . . sit!" said Harry.
"I won't be long."
And then he was gone.
"Why are you sitting there?" asked a nosy bird. "Are you going to sit there all day?"

The most obedient dog in the world didn't answer. He just sat and waited for Harry.
Big, fat raindrops began to fall.
"I'm leaving," said the bird. And he flew away.
Everyone ran for cover, except the most obedient dog in the world. Thunder rumbled, lightning flashed, and then the hailstones fell—

lots and lots of hailstones!
When the sun came out again the bird flew back. The most obedient dog in the world was still sitting there waiting for Harry.

IN THE WORLD by Anita Jeram

"What a strange dog," people said as they passed. Other dogs came to take a look. They sniffed and nuzzled and nudged and nipped, but they soon got bored and went away. The most obedient dog in the world sat . . . and sat . . . and sat . . . and sat. How long must he wait for Harry? Just then, a cat came by.

"Quick!" said the bird, pulling his tail. "Why don't you chase it?" The dog's eyes followed the cat. His nose started to twitch, and his legs started to itch. He couldn't sit still any longer. He sprang to his feet . . .

and saw Harry!

"Good boy!" said Harry. "You waited! Leave that cat. Let's go to the beach!"

The dog looked at the cat, and he looked at Harry. Then he went to the beach with Harry. After all, he was . . .

the most obedient dog in the world!

A PIECE of STRING

IS A WONDERFUL THING

Let us sing a song
about string—
what a wonderful thing it is!
When you think of the things
that you do with string,
you have to admit
it's a marvelous bit
to have in your kit:
for a fishing line, a boat, a kite,
somewhere to hang your socks to dry;
for tying up packages, fastening gates,
leading you safe through a
treacherous cave;
for a spinning top, a skipping rope,
a bracelet, a necklace,
a drawstring purse . . .
there's just about no end of things
a person can do with a piece of string!
And then you wonder,
from time to time,
how did a thing like
string begin?
Back in the days
when mammoths roamed,
and they didn't have chains
and they didn't have ropes
for hauling around
or lifting things up—

(well, they didn't have
any connecting things:
buttons or braces or buckles or laces,
or latches or catches or bolts or belts,
or tabs or clasps or hooks and eyes . . .
Velcro patches! ribbons! ties!
zips or grips or snaps or clips)—
well how did anyone
THINK IT UP?
Did they chat as they sat
near the fire at night,
eating their prehistoric fish,
and say, "What we need
to get it right
is a thing like hair,
but long and strong,
a thing to tie on a piece of bone:
what a wonderful fishing line
that would make!"?
After which, I suppose,
they went out to the lake
and tickled the fish
with their cold, bare hands—
for they didn't have nets
if they didn't have string.
How they all must have wished
that they had such a thing!

24

← slip knot

A slip knot can hitch
a boat, a horse,
a swing . . .

three small knots   three big knots   three small knots

≡ ... --- ...
≡ Morse code for S.O.S.

My friend's uncle said,
change for a phone call.

by Judy Hindley   illustrated by Margaret Chamberlain

So how on earth
do you think they discovered it?
Do you think somebody
just tripped over it?
Was it an accident?
Was it a guess?
Did it emerge
from a hideous mess?
Did it begin with
a sinuous twig,
a whippety willow,
a snaky vine?
Did it happen that somebody,
one dark night,
winding his weary way
home alone,
got tripped by the foot
on a loop of a vine
and fell kersplat! and bust a bone;
and then, as he lay in the dark, so sad,
and yelled for help (and it didn't come)
he got thoroughly bored with doing that
and invented—
a woolly-rhinoceros trap?

Oh, it might have occurred
in a number of ways
as the populace pondered
the fate they faced—
as they huddled in caves
in the worst of the weather,
wishing for things like
tents and clothes,
as they hugged furry skins
to their shivery bodies
and scraps of hide
to their cold, bare toes.
And they had no suspenders
or snaps or connectors
or buttons or toggles
or zippers or pins—
so HOW did they hold up
their trousers, then?
They must have said,
"Oh! a piece of string
would be SUCH a fine thing
to have around the cave!"

"You should never go anywhere without a pencil stub, and a piece of string."

For a long time the only spears were pointed sticks.
Much later, a chip of stone would be tied to
the stick with a sinew.

25

They needed a noose
for an antelope foot.
They needed a thing to string a bow.

And they spun out the fibers
of vegetable fluff,
and they felted the hairs of a goat,
and they knitted and twisted
and braided and twined
and invented . . .

A single fiber of wool is as strong as a thread of gold.

Things on strings are a glamorous way to deck your body.

They needed nets,
and traps, and snares
for catching their venison unaware
and leading the first wild horses home.

Well, they must've gone on
to try and try
as hundreds of thousands
of years went by,
twisting and braiding and trying out knots
with strips of hide and rhinoceros guts,
spiders' webs and liana vines,
reeds and weeds and ribs of palm,
slippery sinews, muscles, and thongs,
elephant grasses three feet long,
and wriggly fish-bone skeletons.

the three-ply rope!
What a wonderful thing!
A very fine thing!
The KING of string is rope!
You can lift up pots
from an echoing well with it,
fling it to make a bridge;
you can haul along
hulking hunks of stone
for building a pyramid
(and they did).
You can also halter and harness
your animal friends.
  And then again, when life gets tough
    and it's time to be moving along,

One hunting breakthrough was the bolas — three stones tied to a leather strap or a sinew.

you can use it to lash your luggage fast
to a camel, a goat,
  a raft, a boat—

Think of necklaces, pendants,
  belts, and bracelets.

oh! a stringable thing
is the only thing
to have when you're afloat!

But they still
went on and on,
sticking and spinning
and looping and gluing
and tying and trying out
more and more types,
quicker and quicker
crazier, slicker
for pulleys and ladders
and hoses and bridges
and fences and winches
and wires and pipes.

Where on earth
have we come to now?

What would a town
ever do without string
and things that go stringing along?
Candlewicks, rackets, and violins,
telephones, plumbing, and railroad
lines, things that fasten and fuse and fix
and click and stick and link.
Can you even begin
to count the ways
that things connect
with other things?
It could just about
scramble your brain!
And to think it began
(though we'll never know when)
with somebody choking
on elephant gristle,
or trying to chew
through the stem of a thistle,
or just stumbling into the thing!
Oh, what we've done
with a piece of string
is a marvelous thing,
an amazing thing—
some would say
a crazy thing!
And one of these days
I might just go away
and begin it
all over
again . . .

27

CUPBOARD BEAR

by Jez Alborough

But what a shock—when he gets there,
the ice cream's gone, the cupboard's bare!

Bear should fix that broken pane—
it dribbles drops of snow and rain.

As he turns and starts to shout,
a pile of snow falls on his snout.
At least, that is, he
thinks it's snow.
It feels too thick
and sticky though,
and tastes like sugar.
Can it mean . . .

But jobs like that are always kept
till after lazy Bear has slept.

He dreams of slipping out the back
to get himself an icy snack.

it's snowing blobs of white ice cream? It's twice as
nice as snow or ice— it's Bear's idea of paradise.

Before he tries to eat it all, he makes himself a little ball, then rolls it into something grand—

But suddenly it starts to slip,

the biggest scoop in all the land!

and Bear begins to lose his grip.

Now it's time without delay . . .

to make a speedy getaway. He sees a rock too late to dodge, rolls over once and . . .

WATCH OUT!

SPLODGE!

"Ice cream!" he screams. "Ice cream, ice cream! Thank heavens, it was all a dream."

Now he does not hesitate— the household chores will have to wait. Broken windows should be fixed . . . but work and pleasure *can't* be mixed.

FARMER DUCK

by **Martin Waddell** *illustrated by* **Helen Oxenbury**

There once was a duck who had the bad luck to live with a lazy old farmer. The duck did the work. The farmer stayed all day in bed. The duck fetched the cow from the field.

"How goes the work?" called the farmer.

The duck answered,

"Quack!"

The duck brought the sheep from the hill.

"How goes the work?" called the farmer.

The duck answered,

"Quack!"

The duck put the hens in their house.

"How goes the work?" called the farmer.

The duck answered,

"Quack!"

The farmer got fat through staying in bed, and the poor duck got fed up with working all day.

"How goes the work?"

"Quack!"

"How goes the work?"
"Quack!"

"How goes the work?"
"Quack!"

The poor duck grew
sleepy and weepy
and tired.
The hens and
the cow and the
sheep got very upset.
They loved the duck.
So they held a meeting under the
moon, and they made a plan for the
morning.

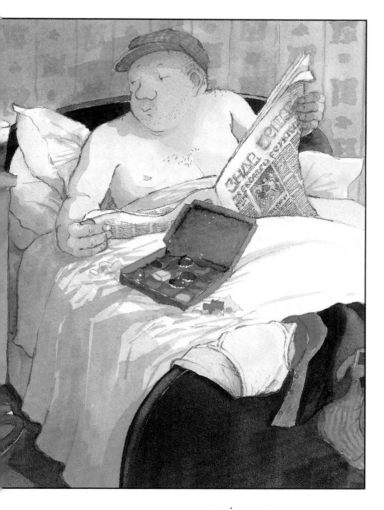

"How goes the work?"
"Quack!"

"How goes the work?"
"Quack!"

"How goes the work?"
"Quack!"

"Moo!" said the cow.
"Baa!" said the sheep.
"Cluck!" said the hens.

And *that* was the plan!

31

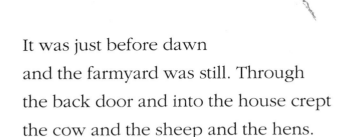

It was just before dawn
and the farmyard was still. Through
the back door and into the house crept
the cow and the sheep and the hens.

They stole down the hall.
They creaked up the stairs.
They squeezed under
the bed of the farmer
and wriggled about.
The bed started to rock
and the farmer woke up,
and he called,
"How goes the work?" and . . .

"**M o o!**"

"**B a a!**"

"**C l u c k!**"

They lifted his bed
and he started to shout, and
they banged and they bounced
the old farmer about and about and
about, right out of the bed . . .
and he fled with the cow and the
sheep and the hens mooing and
baaing and clucking behind him.

The duck awoke and waddled wearily into the yard expecting to hear, "How goes the work?" But nobody spoke!

Then the cow and the sheep and the hens came back.

"**Quack?**" asked the duck.

"**Moo!**" said the cow.

"**Baa!**" said the sheep.

"**Cluck!**" said the hens.

Down the lane . . . "**Moo!**"

through the fields . . . "**Baa!**"

over the hill . . . "**Cluck!**"

and he never came back.

Which told the duck the whole story.

Then mooing and baaing and clucking and quacking they all set to work on their farm.

THE BOY WHO CRIED WOLF

FROM
THE BEST OF AESOP'S FABLES

A boy was sent to tend a flock of sheep as they grazed near a village. It was raining, and he was bored, so he decided to play a trick on the villagers.

"Wolf! Wolf!" he shouted as loud as he could. "There's a wolf attacking your sheep."

Out ran all the villagers, leaving whatever they were doing, to drive away the wolf. When they rushed into the field and found the sheep quite safe, the boy laughed and laughed. The next day the same thing happened.

Retold by
Margaret Clark

Illustrated by
Charlotte Voake

"Wolf! Wolf!" shouted the boy.
And when the villagers
ran into the field and
again found
everything quiet, he
laughed more than ever.
On the third day a wolf
really did come.
"Wolf! Wolf!"
shouted the boy, as the sheep
ran wildly in all directions.
"Oh, please come quickly!"
But this time the villagers ignored
him, because they thought he
was only playing tricks, as he
had done before.

35

Phew, Waldo-watchers, here's one of the mega-trickiest Waldo searches ever!

Can you find the real Waldo?
(*He's only wearing one shoe!*)

Can you find Waldo's other shoe?

Can you find Waldo's lost key?

Can you find Wenda?

Can you find Woof? (*All you can see is his tail!*)

Last of all, O brilliant, brainy ones, how many characters can you find who are not Waldos at all?

The FIBBS
by Chris Riddell

"Did you get the bananas?" asked Mrs. Fibb
when Mr. Fibb got back from the store.
"Well, no," said Mr. Fibb. "I meant to, but . . ."
"But what?" said Mrs. Fibb.
"You're never going to believe this," said Mr. Fibb,
"but I had just come out of the grocery store . . .

when a giant hairy hand came down from the
sky and grabbed me! There I was on top of a
skyscraper in the clutches of a giant gorilla. I could see
police cars and fire engines down below, and a huge crowd
gathered. Then from out of the clouds
came fighter planes with their guns
blazing, and the gorilla got very
angry. So before anything nasty
happened I decided to try to fix things myself.
'Excuse me,' I said to the gorilla, 'would
you care for a banana?'
'How kind,' said the gorilla, and ate all the
bananas in one mouthful. Then he gave
me a ride home on his back.
"But never mind, we can have
some of your chocolate cake instead."
"Well, no," said Mrs. Fibb. "I was baking today, but . . . "
"But what?" said Mr. Fibb.
"*You're never going to believe this,*" said Mrs. Fibb,
"but just after you left, something that looked
like a giant tea saucer landed in the backyard.

And three little green people climbed
out of it and came into the kitchen.
'We come in peace, earth woman,' they said.
'What's cooking?'
'Nothing yet,' I said, 'but I'm
about to bake a chocolate cake.'
'Then we will help you,' they said, and right away they began.
'They mixed up flour and baked beans and dishwashing soap and
pepper and put it in the oven. Before you could say 'little green

Martians' the oven door opened
and a big spongy blob
jumped out and started
chasing the cat.
'That's the best cake
we've ever baked,' said
the little green people.
'You can keep it if you want.'
'No, thank you,' I said.
'I like earth cooking much
better.' So then I baked them
a big chocolate cake.

When they had all tasted a piece, they said,
'You must give us the recipe, earth woman.'
'Only if you take that nasty blob with you
when you go,' I replied. So they did. And I'm
sorry, but they took the rest of the chocolate cake.
But, never mind, at least we can have a cup of tea.
"Now where's the teapot?"

"You're never going to believe this,"

said Tommy Fibb, running into the room, "but . . ."

"But what?" said Mr. and Mrs. Fibb.

"Well," said Tommy Fibb, "Mrs. McBean

from next door accidentally kicked her soccer

ball through the window this morning . . . and it landed on

the table and smashed the teapot. I meant to tell you earlier, but . . ."

"You can't believe a word that child says," said Mrs. Fibb.

"I don't know where he gets it from,"
said Mr. Fibb.

slam bang

go

zoom

swerve

honk

TRANSYLVANIA DREAMING

In the middle of the night
When you're safe in bed
And the doors are locked
And the cats are fed
And it's much too bright
And sleep won't come
And there's something wrong
And you want your mom
And you hear a noise
And you see a shape
And it looks like a bat
Or a man in a cape
And you dare not breathe
And your heart skips a beat
And you're cold as ice
From your head to your feet
And you say a prayer
And you swear to be good
And you'd run for your life
If you only could
And your eyes are wide
And stuck on stalks
As the thing in black

Toward you walks
And the room goes dark
And you faint clean away
And you don't wake up
Till the very next day . . .

And you open your eyes
And the sun is out
And you jump out of bed
And you sing and shout,
"It was only a dream!"
And you dance around the room
And your heart is as light
As a helium balloon
And your mom rushes in
And says, "Hold on a sec . . .

What are those two little
Holes in your neck?"

FRANKENSTEIN

by Colin McNaughton

An excerpt from

Grape Zoo

by Ivor Cutler *illustrated by Jill Barton*

"Mom, I can make walls out of air," Belle said quietly, spitting out a papaya seed onto her spoon.

"How, my little linnet?" asked her mom. She hooked a clothespin over each ear and leaned forward, a sure sign that she was listening.

"Look! I just squash it hard between my hands—like this!" Belle said, and passed her a fresh piece of air wall.

"Wow!" breathed Mrs. Grape, and the clothespins fell onto the floor among some seeds that had missed the spoon.

Belle worked all afternoon squashing air between two wooden boards till there were two big piles. Then she went in for dinner.

"Mom, will you get Maisie the Wise on the phone, please?" she mumbled, her mouth full of scrambled egg and toast.

Pansy dialed the number. "Hello, Maisie—Belle Grape to speak to you. Here, Belle!" She handed her the phone.

Belle flicked a crumb from her lip onto her plate. "Hello, Maisie the Wise. Would you like me to build you a worm and fly zoo using air walls? You are the first person I've asked."

The wise woman gasped. "Air walls! Do you know what you're doing, Belle Grape?"

"I've tested them, Maisie the Wise. They have the Belle Grape sign of approval—an elephant sitting on a grape."

"Okay, Belle. Build me a worm and fly zoo."

"Right away, Maisie the Wise, and thank you for your order. You won't be sorry. Good-bye!"

My Old Teddy

by
DOM MANSELL

My old Teddy's ear came off.
Poor old Teddy!
I took him to the Teddy doctor.
She made Teddy better.

My old Teddy's leg came off.
Poor old Teddy!
I took him to the Teddy doctor.
She made Teddy better.

My old Teddy's
arm came off.
*Poor old
Teddy!*

I took him to the Teddy doctor.
She made Teddy better.

Then poor old Teddy's head
came off.

48

The Teddy doctor said, "Teddy's had enough now. Teddy has to rest."

The Teddy doctor gave me . . . a new Teddy. I love my new Teddy very much, but I love poor old Teddy best.

Dear old, *poor old* Teddy.

49

But Daedalus hit on a clever plan—he and Icarus would fly like birds away from Crete.

Using feathers bound with wax and twine, he made them both a pair of wonderful wings.

As he fixed Icarus's wings to his back, Daedalus warned his son:

"Do not fly too close to the sea or your wings will get wet,

nor too close to the sun, or the wax will melt."

Then Daedalus and Icarus rose into the air and flew away.

People below were amazed. They thought they must be seeing gods.

At first Icarus stayed close behind his father,

but soon he was overwhelmed with the joy of flying.

Higher and higher he rose,

closer and closer to the sun . . .

until its
hot brilliance
surrounded
him.

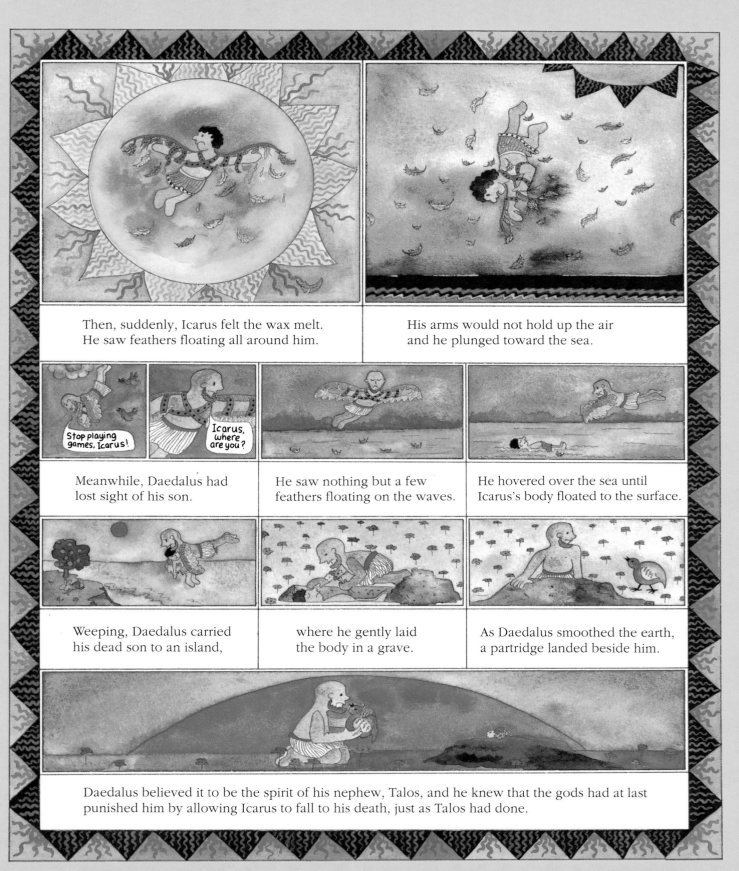

Then, suddenly, Icarus felt the wax melt.
He saw feathers floating all around him.

His arms would not hold up the air
and he plunged toward the sea.

Stop playing games, Icarus!

Icarus, where are you?

Meanwhile, Daedalus had
lost sight of his son.

He saw nothing but a few
feathers floating on the waves.

He hovered over the sea until
Icarus's body floated to the surface.

Weeping, Daedalus carried
his dead son to an island,

where he gently laid
the body in a grave.

As Daedalus smoothed the earth,
a partridge landed beside him.

Daedalus believed it to be the spirit of his nephew, Talos, and he knew that the gods had at last
punished him by allowing Icarus to fall to his death, just as Talos had done.

Tongue Twisters

Betty Botter bought some butter,
But, she said, the butter's bitter;
If I put it in my batter
It will make my batter bitter,
But a bit of better butter
Will make my batter better.
So she bought a bit of butter
Better than her bitter butter,
And she put it in her batter
And the batter was not bitter.
So 'twas better Betty Botter
Bought a bit of better butter.

Moses supposes his toeses are roses,
But Moses supposes erroneously;
For nobody's toeses are posies of roses
As Moses supposes his toeses to be.

54

How much wood would a woodchuck chuck
If a woodchuck could chuck wood?
He would chuck as much wood as a
woodchuck could chuck
If a woodchuck could chuck wood.

Peter Piper picked a peck of pickled peppers;
A peck of pickled peppers Peter Piper picked.
If Peter Piper picked a peck of pickled peppers,
Where's the peck of pickled peppers
Peter Piper picked?

Swan swam over the sea.
Swim, swan, swim!
Swan swam back again.
Well swum, swan!

Little Pig's Tale

by
Nigel Gray

illustrated by
Mary Rees

On Monday, Little Pig's dad told him, "Next Sunday, it's your mom's birthday."

"Will she have a party?" asked Little Pig.

"No. I don't think she'll have a party," said Dad.

"Will she have a birthday cake with lots of candles?"

"No. I don't think she'll want a cake with lots of candles."

"Will we sing 'Happy Birthday to You'?"

"Yes. We must sing 'Happy Birthday to You.'"

"And will we give her presents?"

"Of course," said Dad. "I'll give her a present. And you should give her a present too."

"What will I give her?" asked Little Pig.

"I don't know," said Dad. "You'll have to think of something."

On Tuesday, Little Pig tried to think of something exciting. Perhaps his mom would like an airplane so she could fly high, high above the town . . . or a rocket so she could explore the moon . . . or a spaceship so she could venture into outer space. But Little Pig knew he couldn't really give her a spaceship, or a rocket, or even an airplane. For one thing, their garage was too small. He'd have to think of something else.

On Wednesday, Little Pig thought of flowers and fruit. He'd give his mom an orchard—an orchard with pears and plums, apples and apricots, with daffodils and crocuses growing in the lush grass under the trees. He knew she'd like that because she was always weeding her window box, and growing plants in pots from apple seeds and cherry pits.

Little Pig went to see Mr. Green, the gardener. "I'm sure your mom would love an orchard," said Mr. Green, "but your backyard is too small, and trees take years to grow. It was a good idea, Little Pig, but I'm afraid you'll have to think of something else."

On Thursday, Little Pig knew what he had to do. He raided his piggybank and took his pennies to the store.

He would buy his mom a silk gown, and a warm coat, and shiny shoes, and furry gloves, and glittering jewels for her to wear around her neck.

But the storekeeper counted Little Pig's pennies and said, "I'm sorry, Little Pig, but you don't have enough money for any of those things."

"Not even for the gloves?" asked Little Pig.

"Not even for one glove," said the storekeeper.

On Friday, Little Pig felt sad. In two days it would be his mom's birthday and Little Pig had nothing to give her. What was he to do?

He asked his dad.

"Why don't you make her something?" suggested Dad.

So Little Pig set to work.

He'd make her a useful box for keeping things in.

He got the tools and found some old pieces of wood in the shed. The wood splintered. The box broke.

He'd make her a beautiful necklace of beads. He got the beads from the odds and ends drawer and threaded them together. The thread snapped and the beads spilled all over the floor.

He'd do a painting in rainbow colors.

He got out the paints and a large sheet of white paper. But he knocked over the jar of black paint and ruined his painting with an ugly blotch.

He'd bake some muffins.

He mixed up flour and milk and eggs and raisins and dates, and greased the baking tray with margarine. But the muffins burned and came out of the oven as hard as stones.

On Saturday, Little Pig was in despair. He thought and thought until his brain hurt.

And then he had a brain wave.

He gathered together the things he would need.

A piece of paper, a pen, and a red ribbon.

On Sunday, it was Little Pig's mom's birthday. After breakfast Little Pig and Dad sang "Happy Birthday to You." Then Dad gave Mom a present . . .

and while no one was looking, Little Pig slipped away.

Mom unwrapped her package. Inside was a watch.

"That's because I want you to have a good time," Dad said. And Mom gave Dad a kiss.

Then, on the table, Mom found a note. It said:

To Mom:

Your present is upstairs in your bed.
Happy Birthday!
Lots of love from Little Pig.

Mom went up to the bedroom. There was certainly something in the bed. She pulled back the covers and there was . . .

Little Pig, with a red ribbon tied around him in a bow. "Happy Birthday, Mom!" said Little Pig.

"Oh, Little Pig," said Mom, "this is the best present you could possibly have given me. There's nothing in the world I'd rather have."

Mom hugged Little Pig and gave him a big sloppy kiss. And Little Pig beamed from ear to ear.

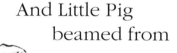

Noah's Ark

A long time ago there lived a man called Noah.

Noah was a good man, who trusted in God.

There were also many wicked people in the world.

God wanted to punish the wicked people,

so he said to Noah,

"I shall make a flood of water and wash all the wicked people away. Build an ark for your family and all the animals."

Noah worked for years and years and years to build the ark.

At last the ark was finished.

Noah and his family gathered lots of food.

Then the animals came,

two by two,

two by two,

into the ark.

by Lucy Cousins

When the ark was full, Noah felt a drop of rain. It rained and rained and rained. It rained for forty days and forty nights. The world was covered with water. At last the rain stopped and the sun came out. Noah sent a dove to find dry land. The dove came back with a leafy twig. "Hurrah!" shouted Noah. "The flood has ended." But many more days passed before the ark came to rest on dry land. Then Noah and all the animals came safely out of the ark . . . and life began again on the earth.

61

DUDLEY
AND THE
STRAWBERRY SHAKE

PETER CROSS
Text by JUDY TAYLOR

There was a soft breeze blowing in Shadyhanger and it carried the scent of strawberries through the open window.

Dudley had been awake since early morning searching for his special gloves. Today he was going strawberry picking.

The sun was shining strongly and the ground felt warm.

Dudley set off with his berry barrow down the lane to the strawberry patch. Long before he got there, his mouth was watering.

As he turned the corner, there, they were before him— row upon row of fat, juicy strawberries.

Dudley picked a big strawberry very carefully with his special gloves.

He took a bite to see if it was ripe. It was.

He took another bite just to make sure . . . and another and another . . .

until there was nothing left.

Dudley was very full.

Just then, over by the hedge, Dudley spied an extra large strawberry, the largest he had ever seen.

"That's the one I'll take home for lunch," he said.

Dudley gripped the strawberry firmly with his gloves, but it wouldn't come.

He tried again, pulling and pulling with all his might.

Suddenly the strawberry began to shake violently.

Dudley hung on until he felt his hands slipping out of his gloves.

Then he was sailing through the air. He landed on the grass with a *bump!*

"What an odd strawberry," thought Dudley, feeling a little dizzy.

Dudley waited until the world had stopped spinning around.

"It feels like nap time," he said, hurrying home.

And just as he was drifting off to sleep, Dudley remembered he had left his gloves behind.

An excerpt from

CRUMBANG CASTLE

by Sarah Hayes illustrated by Helen Craig

A minute before midnight the little ghost felt her usual shivering feeling. "Time to go to work," she said. The moon was shining brightly, and the ghost was no more than a faint haze against the darkest part of the sky. She floated down from the bell tower, wailing gently. Halfway down, a lump of stone dislodged itself from the wall and went crashing down the steps. It made a tremendous noise in the silence, but the little ghost did not seem to hear it. She lingered in the marble hall and shrieked as horribly as she could. Anyone listening would have thought it was the wind whistling, for over the years the little ghost's voice had grown very faint.

Through the marble hall she went, across the ballroom where a large spider sat in a pool of moonlight, and into the long corridor. The wizard was nowhere around, but the little ghost opened and closed a few doors anyway because that was what she did every night. When she reached the battlements, she paused. Zeb was in his favorite position, leaning against the wall looking up at the sky. On fine nights he often stood there for an hour or more, gazing at the stars. Tonight, however, he threw out his hands and nodded happily as several small sparks came from his fingertips.

There were others besides the little ghost who were watching the wizard practice finger lightning. Up in the tower sat two birds, perched on the great bell. Jason, the wizard's crow, was trying not to laugh, and the owl, who had been out hunting, was sitting hunched up with closed eyes, paying no attention to what was going on below.

Somewhere a slate crashed to the ground. The castle shook slightly, and the little ghost began to glide toward the wizard. Jason peered down from the tower. The owl opened her eyes a slit. The shadowy outline of the ghost reached the wizard. Zeb shivered and pulled his cloak around his shoulders.

Then the little ghost saw the beetle.

Nestling in the bent tip of the wizard's hat, waving his feelers slightly, sat the largest, blackest, most terrifying beetle the ghost had ever seen. She screamed. She screamed a scream that tore across the sky and froze the water in the streams for miles around. The wizard fell backward. Rigid with terror, Jason watched from his perch on the bell. He saw the ghost grow thick and white. Then he saw the huge beetle open its wings and fly up over the battlements. The scream came again and again.

The crow and the owl toppled off their perches, and the great bell swung. For the first time in a hundred years, the rusty clapper clanged. The bell rang hollowly. Jason and the owl began to plummet to the ground.

The ghost screamed again and again. The toads in the basement tried to hide under each other. The spider lay on her back in the pool of moonlight on the ballroom floor. The rats and mice and bats stopped squeaking. Only the giant beetle moved. It flew calmly on, down toward the basement. Its job was done.

As for the ghost, she was now a fearsome figure, and her white trails stretched the whole length of the battlements. Zeb opened his eyes. At first he thought a fog had come down over the castle. Then he saw two great black holes glaring at him, and the swirling trails of mist. "A phantom," he whispered, and fainted.

67

EAT

YOUR DINNER!

BY VIRGINIA MILLER

George came looking for
Bartholomew with his dinner.
"Dinner's ready, Ba," he said.
"Have you washed your face
and hands?"

"Nah!" said Bartholomew.

George said, "Sit up, Ba,
and eat your dinner."

"Nah, nah, nah,
nah, NAH!"
said Bartholomew.

"Eat your dinner!"
George said in a big voice.

Bartholomew ate one
spoonful, then he had
a little rest.

George sat down at
the table and began to
eat his dinner.

Bartholomew watched until
George had finished.

Then George left the table
and returned with a large
honey cake.

He cut a slice and ate it.
When he had finished,
he took the rest away.

Suddenly
Bartholomew thought,

Eat your dinner!

He thought of the
honey cake . . .
with the pretty pink icing . . .

and the cherry on top . . .

and he licked his bowl
perfectly clean.

He went to find George.

"You've finished, Ba!"
George said.

"Nah," said Bartholomew.
George smiled and gave
him the slice of cake with
the cherry on top.

Nah

An excerpt from

THE FINGER-EATER

by
DICK KING-SMITH

illustrated by
ARTHUR ROBINS

Long long ago, in the cold lands of the North, there lived a most unusual troll.

Like all the hill-folk (so called because they usually made their homes in holes in the hills) he was humpbacked and bow-legged, with a frog-face and bat-ears and razor-sharp teeth.

But he grew up (though, like all other trolls, not very tall) with an extremely bad habit—he liked to eat fingers!

Ulf (for that was his name) always went about this in the same way. Whenever he spied someone walking alone in the hills, he would come up, smiling broadly, and hold out a

72

would carry him, chewing like mad and grinning all over his frog-face.

Strangers visiting those parts were amazed to see how many men, women, and children were lacking a finger on their right hand, especially children, because their fingers were tenderer and much sought after by Ulf.

hand, and say politely, "How do you do?"

Now trolls are usually rude and extremely grumpy and don't care how anyone does, so the person would be pleasantly surprised at meeting such a friendly one, and would hold out his or her hand to shake Ulf's.

Then Ulf would take it and, quick as a flash, bite off a finger with his razor-sharp teeth and run away as fast as his bowlegs

73

Oh, Little Jack

by Inga Moore

It was a windy day. Little Jack Rabbit went into the garden. Mommy was in her vegetable patch. She was pulling up onions. "Can I help?" asked Little Jack. Little Jack Rabbit found an onion with a brown curly top. He tugged and he tugged. He tugged as hard as he could. But he couldn't pull it out of the ground.

"Oh, Little Jack!" said Mommy. "I think you are too small to pull up onions."

In the garden the wind was blowing down the leaves. "I will have to sweep up these leaves," said Daddy.

"Can I do it?" asked Little Jack. Little Jack Rabbit ran to get the broom. But the broom was very long. He couldn't make it sweep. "Oh, Little Jack!" said Daddy. "I think you are too small to sweep up leaves."

Little Jack Rabbit went to the park with his sister Nancy and his big brother Buck. Buck flew his new blue kite.

"Can I fly it?" asked Little Jack.
Little Jack Rabbit held the kite
by its string. He held it as tightly
as he could. But the wind pulled
and pulled. It nearly pulled
the kite away.

"Oh, Little Jack!" said Buck.
"I think you are too small to
fly a kite."
On the way home Nancy rode
her go-cart down the hill.
"Can I have a turn?" asked Little
Jack.
Little Jack Rabbit sat in the
go-cart.
He rode
it down
the hill.
But he couldn't
make it stop
at the
bottom.

"Oh, Little
Jack!" said
Nancy.
"I think you
are too small
to ride in a
go-cart."

At home, Little Jack Rabbit went into the kitchen. His sisters Rhona and Rita were helping Mommy make tea. She was going to take some to Granpa.

"Can I take it?" asked Little Jack. Little Jack Rabbit picked up the cup. He carried it as carefully as he could. But he spilt the tea into the saucer.

"Oh, Little Jack!" said Rita.

"I think you are too small to carry a cup of tea."

Poor Little Jack Rabbit ran to find his granpa.

"What's the matter, Little Jack?" Granpa asked.

"I am too small," said Little Jack.

"Too small for what?" asked Granpa.

"I am too small for everything," said Little Jack.

Granpa had been busy in his workshop.

He had been fixing something. It was a little red tricycle.

"Who is it for?" asked Little Jack.

"It can't be for me," said Mommy. "I am too big. And it can't be for Daddy. He's *much* too big."

"Is it for Buck?" asked Little Jack.

No, the tricycle was not for Buck. It was not for Nancy or Rhona or Rita. They were all too big to ride it.

"Can I ride it?" asked Little Jack.

It was better than flying a kite. It was even better than riding in a go-cart. And it was much better than carrying a cup of tea. "Thank you, Granpa," said Little Jack.

That night Little Jack Rabbit sat by the fire with his family. Now he was glad he was small. And not only because of the little red tricycle. There was something else, something he had forgotten. He was just the right size to sit on Granpa's knee.

Little Jack Rabbit climbed onto the little red tricycle. He was not too big, and he was not too small. "Why, Little Jack!" said Granpa. "You are just the right size. The tricycle must be for you." Little Jack Rabbit rode his little red tricycle around and around the garden. It was better than pulling up onions or sweeping leaves.

SILLY GOOSE

I swing like a gibbon.

I hop like a flea.

I jump like a kangaroo.

I paddle like a duck.

I flap like a bat.

I parade like a peacock.

I hide my head like an ostrich.

by Jan Ormerod

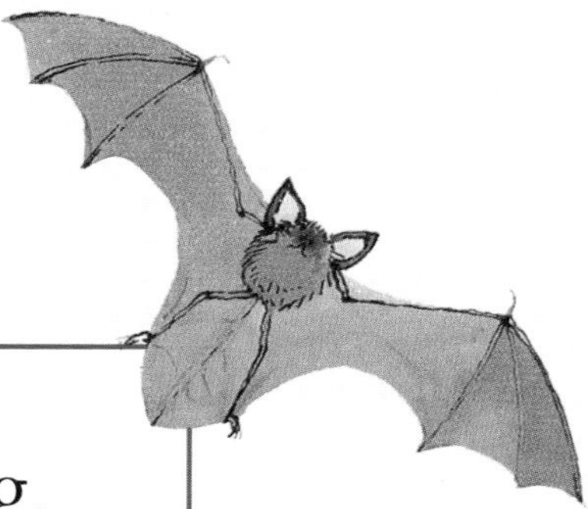

Swinging. Hopping. Jumping.

Paddling. Flapping. Parading.

Hiding my head.

Sometimes I'm just
as silly as a goose.

79

ALICE'S ADVENTURES IN WONDERLAND

by Lewis Carroll illustrated by Anthony Browne

"**R**epeat *'You are old, Father William,'*" said the Caterpillar.

Alice folded her hands, and began:

" '*You are old, Father William,' the young man said,
'And your hair has become very white;
And yet you incessantly stand on your head –
Do you think, at your age, it is right?'*

*'In my youth,' Father William replied to his son,
'I feared it might injure the brain;
But, now that I'm perfectly sure I have none,
Why, I do it again and again.'*

*'You are old,' said the youth, 'as I mentioned before,
And have grown most uncommonly fat;
Yet you turned a back-somersault in at the door –
Pray, what is the reason of that?'*

*'In my youth,' said the sage, as he shook his grey locks,
'I kept all my limbs very supple
By the use of this ointment – one shilling the box –
Allow me to sell you a couple?'*

*'You are old,' said the youth, 'and your jaws are too weak
For anything tougher than suet;
Yet you finished the goose, with the bones and the beak –
Pray how did you manage to do it?'*

*'In my youth,' said his father, 'I took to the law,
And argued each case with my wife;
And the muscular strength, which it gave to my jaw,
Has lasted the rest of my life.'*

*'You are old,' said the youth, 'one would hardly suppose
That your eye was as steady as ever;
Yet you balanced an eel on the end of your nose –
What made you so awfully clever?'*

*'I have answered three questions, and that is enough,'
Said his father, 'don't give yourself airs!
Do you think I can listen all day to such stuff?
Be off, or I'll kick you downstairs!'* "

"That is not said right," said the Caterpillar.
"Not *quite* right, I'm afraid," said Alice, timidly, "some of the words have got altered."
"It is wrong from beginning to end," said the Caterpillar decidedly.

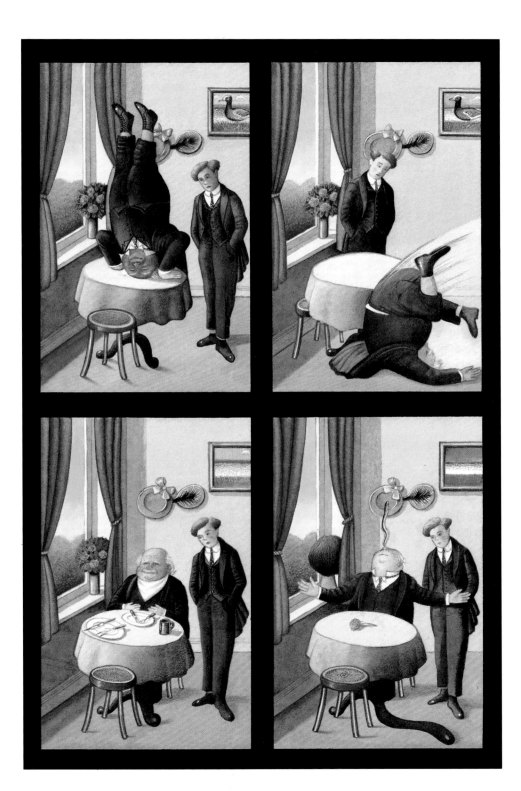

81

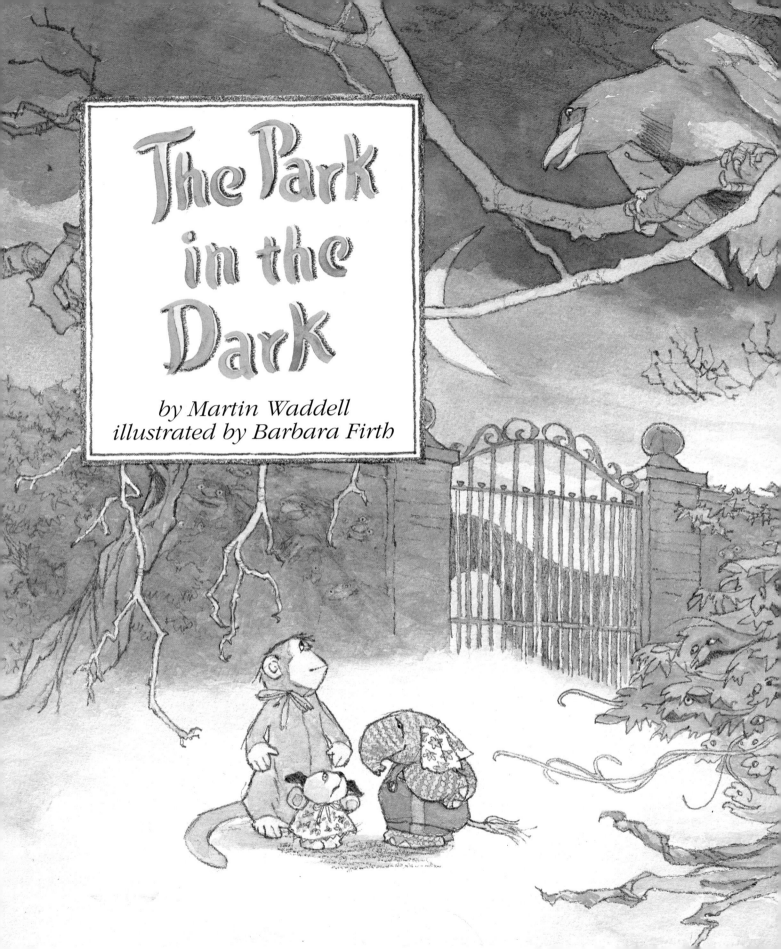

The Park in the Dark

by Martin Waddell
illustrated by Barbara Firth

When the sun goes down
and the moon comes up
and the old swing creaks in the dark,
that's when we go to the park,
   me and Loopy and Little Gee,
   all three.

Softly down the staircase,
through the haunty hall,
trying to look small,
   me and Loopy and Little Gee,
   we three.

It's shivery out in the dark
on our way to the park,
down trash can alley,
past the ruined mill, so still,
   just me and Loopy and Little Gee,
   just three.

And Little Gee doesn't like it.
He's scared of the things he might see
in the park in the dark
with Loopy and me.
   That's me and Loopy and Little Gee,
   the three.

There might be moon witches
or man-eating trees
or withers that wobble
or old Scrawny Shins
or hairy hobgoblins,
or black boggarts' knees in the trees,
or things we can't see,
   me and Loopy and Little Gee,
   all three.

But there aren't, says Loopy,
and I agree,
and Little Gee gets up on my back
and we pass the Howl Tree,
    me and Loopy and Little Gee.
        We're heroes, we three.

In the park in the dark
by the lake and the bridge,
at last we see
where we want to be,
    me and Loopy
        and Little Gee.
            WHOOPEE!

And we swing and we slide
and we dance and we jump
and we chase all over the place,
me and Loopy
    and Little Gee,
        the Big Three!

And then the THING comes!
YAAAAA
AAAIII
OOOOOEEEEEEE!

RUN RUN RUN
shouts Little Gee to Loopy and me
and we flee,
    me and Loopy
        and Little Gee,
            scared three.

Back where we came
through the park in the dark
and the THING is roaring
and following, see?
   After me and Loopy
      and Little Gee,
         we three.

Up to the
house, to the stair,
to the bed where we ought to be,
me and Loopy and Little Gee,
   safe as can be,
      all three.

 JEFFREY STRANGEWAYS

by Jill Murphy

The flames leapt higher and higher, lighting up the curved trees and the mouth of a cave in the rocks. The ogre hurled whole tree trunks onto the fire, its ghastly shadow stretching twice as large up the hillside behind it.

To Jeffrey, crouching in the darkness, it seemed as if he was watching a terrifying scene on a stage. The creature began to grunt and roar as it threw more fuel onto the blazing pyre.

Watching transfixed, Jeffrey had completely forgotten about Lancelot. The roaring of the ogre proved too much for his dizzy puppy brain. Here was his new master beside him, and *there* was a decidedly threatening enemy making decidedly threatening noises. There was no doubt about it in Lancelot's mind: His master needed defending at once.

the end of the flailing rope. Lancelot had continued to twirl around the vast form until the rope tied its ankles together so suddenly that the huge monster toppled backward. There was a terrible thud that shook the whole hillside as the ogre's head struck a rock at the entrance to the cave.

With a bloodcurdling howl, he dashed forward, lips drawn back in as vicious-looking a snarl as he could manage. (Actually it wasn't vicious-looking at all. He was such a sweet-natured dog that it just made him look comical instead of nasty.)

Jeffrey watched in horror as the puppy rushed into the circle of light, barking frenziedly, fur standing on end like a wolf, and with the rope flying out behind him.

He looked so tiny darting around the ogre's ankles that Jeffrey closed his eyes and waited for the barking to be brought to an abrupt end by one of the hairy fists.

Then a wonderful thing happened. Jeffrey cautiously opened one eye and saw that the ogre had trodden on

FLY BY NIGHT

Once, at the edge of the woods, lived two owls, a mother owl and her young one, Blink. Every day, all day long, they slept. Every night, all night long, the mother owl flew and Blink waited.

One day, when the sun was still low in the sky, Blink opened one eye and said, "Now? Is it time?"

"Soon," said his mother. "Soon. Go back to sleep."

Blink tried to sleep. When the sun rose and warmed the earth, he opened the other eye. "*Now* is it time?"

"Not yet," said his mother. "Soon. Go back to sleep."

Blink tried. Butterflies looped and drifted past him. Beetles scuttled in the undergrowth. Nearby, a woodpecker tapped on a tree trunk. Blink couldn't sit still.

"Is it time *yet*?" he said.

His mother opened her eyes. "You are old enough and strong enough . . . "— Blink dithered with excitement—"but you must wait."

His mother closed her eyes.

"Wait for *what*?" Blink wondered.

JUNE CREBBIN *ILLUSTRATED BY* STEPHEN LAMBERT

The sun was at its highest.
A squirrel leapt from tree to
tree, quicker than a thought.
Along Blink's branch it came,
right past him, its tail
streaming out behind.
Blink wriggled and jiggled.
He *couldn't* sit still. All that
long afternoon, he watched
and waited. He shuffled and
fidgeted. Below, in the
clearing, a deer and its fawn
browsed on leaves and twigs.
High above, a falcon
hovered, dipped, and soared
again into the sky.
"When will it be *my* time?"
said Blink to himself.
Toward dusk, a sudden gust
of wind, sweeping through
the woods, lifting leaves on

their branches, seemed to gather
Blink from his branch as if it
would lift him too. "Time to fly,"
it seemed to say. Blink fluffed out
his feathers. He shifted his wings.
But the wind swirled by.
It was all puff and nonsense.

Blink sighed.

He closed his eyes.

The sun slipped behind the
fields. The moon rose pale and
clear. A night breeze stirred.
"Time to fly."
"Puff and nonsense,"
muttered Blink.
"*Time to fly*," said his
mother beside him.
Blink sat up. "Is it?" he said.
"Is it? *Really?*"
The gray dusk had deepened.
Blink heard soft whisperings.
He saw the stars in the sky.
He felt the dampness of the
night air. He knew it was time to fly.
He gathered his strength. He drew
himself up, stretched out his wings,
and lifted into the air. Higher and

farther he flew. Over the woods, over the fields, over the road and the sleeping city. His wing beats strong, Blink flew on. Now he knew what he'd been waiting for. The stars had appeared in the night sky. He had waited because he was meant to fly by night.

BOY

by Paul Manning
illustrated by Nicola Bayley

Early morning, boy yawning.

Bad luck, head stuck.

Boy slopping, cup dropping.

Clothes drying, boy crying.